Diari‹

Tommy N Tollesfon

Professor Jordi Gali made the suggestion that financial exclusion studies might be useful in this area during a workshop that the Spanish Savings Banks held in Salamanca in July 2004.

Customers who contribute to a bank's "value-added" in terms of SWM are specifically targeted. The procedure can be summarized as follows: It is demonstrated that customer valuation has evolved into a strategy for increasing shareholder wealth and income, almost always at the expense of (further) marginalizing the poor and disadvantaged.

Therefore, it appears that this process of deregulation—both de facto and de jure—exacerbates financial exclusion. At the same time, this process is slowed down by financial crises, which are another obvious feature of modern financial systems. Crises in the financial system appear to be a feature of the current development. This may, obviously, be the change stage

(of some significant length) towards some higher request, liberated and 'complete' set of monetary business sectors that is liberated from present

'market disappointments' (like the 'Too huge to fall flat' precept and the absence of a worldwide market in bank corporate control). Recurring financial crises appear to be characteristic of the current financial and economic era, regardless of the probable or hypothesized duration (or even existence) of such a transition phase.

Whenever there is a monetary emergency, there is constantly a result

of some sort of 'trip to quality' and an accentuation on risk decrease by the banking and monetary administrations industry. The resulting effects are described as "abandonment and retreat to a more affluent client base" by Leyshon and Thrift (1993, p. 223). This applies not exclusively to specific client sections, yet additionally to separate geographic regions (purported

'monetary desertification'). Leyshon and Frugality (1995, p. 312) further portray the financial cycle as ... 'progressively exclusionary in

reaction to a monetary emergency established in more significant levels of rivalry

what's more, outrageous degrees of obligation'.

Dymski and Li (2002) show in the geographic writing that in

present day US banking, monetary prohibition is normally connected to a specific arrangement of macrostructural conditions. Dymski and Li, however, concur in the current setting (2002, p. 1): The increased financial competition brought on by globalization and deregulation is unquestionably one factor that contributes to banking strategy shifts and, as a result, financial exclusion. They proceed to contend from their exploration that not all banks have followed the lead of the megabanks in their 'essential shift' towards

underscoring higher worth clients.

The apparent industry norm of this latter "strategic shift" is linked, among other things, to a growing gap between the financial circumstances and options of households with lower incomes and those with higher incomes.

Presently and in the future, a significant portion of the

latter group has instantaneous access to financial information, transactions, and value transfers involving their wealth. These social groups now hold a new kind of power thanks to their newly established status as "global financial citizens." The major commercial banks are increasingly targeting this group as a source of known risk and "value additivity" that is already assured.

This upgraded power is in checked differentiation to those lower-pay

bunches at the opposite finish of the family range. The dynamics of this bank strategic process appear to exacerbate this inherent polarization, and these "un-banked" or "marginally banked" groups appear to have less product information, are not as heavily (if at all) targeted for new products, and have less information about products. We have already talked about how "free market mode" key strategic drivers like deregulation, increasing competition, globalization, and current financial crises seem to make financial exclusion even worse. Securitization and retail disintermediation are two additional important drivers.

The process by which corporate credit intermediation moves out of the banking system and into capital markets is known as securitisation.

The term "retail disintermediation" refers to the process by which savings are moved away from the banking system and into money-market mutual funds and offshore vehicles; The banking system's ability to lend and invest is limited as a result of this procedure. On the other hand, securitization results in a decrease in the demand for lending from commercial banks. From one perspective,

these patterns have underlined the improvement of speculation banking

furthermore, resource the executives techniques by US banks. They have also encouraged banks to reevaluate their core banking business at the same time. In

specific, the banks have looked for better approaches to 'secure in' their clients also, create more gain ('esteem added') from them.

New sorts of store instruments, moving into new areas of loaning,

expanding utilization of ABS (Resource upheld Protections) procedures in loaning,

further developing gamble the executives and hazard relief procedures, and a summed up development towards risk-based valuing portray this new key climate. Dymski and Li (2002, p. 4) stress that from

a client point of view, 'normalization' has been vital in these

recharged US banking techniques in buyer banking. This course of

normalization is additionally constricted by a rising utilization of computerbased innovation to evaluate credit gambles, illuminate advance choice and direct estimating. As the SWM model encourages banks to reduce their staffing (and branching) levels in the pursuit of ever-increasing cost efficiency, local knowledge of staff and discretion become less important. Normalized (productive) clients can be more

effortlessly focused on for strategically pitching a bank's current and new items;

It is simpler to originate and securitize standard loans.

138 Financial Exclusion In this new US market following deregulation, banks' strategies have therefore focused on finding profitable "standardized" customers. There are a number of non-exclusive ways to target these last customer groups. For instance, lower benefit client gatherings

can be supported and assisted with becoming by the bank's; client gatherings

might be looked for in new geographic areas; and/or a bank might combine with another bank or banks. The latter is frequently the quickest method for achieving the desired outcome, which helps to explain the recent wave of bank mergers in the United States and the growing dominance of a few megabanks over banking markets.

According to Dymski and Li (2002, p. 5): "mergers and acquisitions are central to the dynamic of the standardised customer" in contemporary US banking. They portray pre-liberation US banking as generally low fixed financial expenses and high minor expenses of overhauling

clients. The new megabanking phase after

deregulation is characterized by low marginal costs for customer service and high fixed costs for product design, testing, and marketing. The primary objective is to target the most profitable customer groups, cultivate these relationships over time, and increasingly target them for a wider range of "value-adding" products.

The essential financial matters of this interaction,

then, at that point, recommend that the standard business banks progressively 'desert' the less productive family gatherings. The resulting financial exclusion has an inevitable geographic (as well as social and economic) spatial dimension due to the fact that these latter, poorer groups frequently cluster in particular geographical locations (parts of a city or a region). We have additionally seen before that where standard monetary administrations are not accessible, different choices can

furthermore, do create to 'fill the holes'. However, this kind of "financial desertification" may prevent further financial and economic development efforts. Dymski and Li (2002) ask if the experiences of ethnobanking in Los Angeles, which took place under very specific macrostructural conditions, point to a possible solution to financial exclusion or, rather, if they are just "the exception that proves the rule."

Thus, the experiences of the "free market model" that followed deregulation in the United States and the United Kingdom appear to provide some interesting, though troubling, insights.

The main point seems to be that the problem of financial exclusion may get worse without the free market model. At the very least, it appears to exacerbate the polarization of societal groups with and without financial resources. As risk-based pricing gets more sophisticated, the free market model may also see an increase in the number of groups excluded (sub-segments). The unchecked free European Policy on Financial Exclusion and Bank Strategies 139 market model is not a solution, just like competition. It appears that a "partnership approach" and "intervention" to financial exclusion are required.

In this context, "intervention" refers to any set of actions that an unregulated private sector company would typically avoid taking. These actions range from "self regulation" by the industry itself to government edicts (affirmative action).

'Self guideline' in this setting covers those financial sub-areas

(whether secretly, commonly or state-claimed) whose essential mission

was the improvement of their districts, helping more unfortunate areas of the

client base and supporting social works. There is no doubt that a lot of these institutions have been motivated to make more money, work more efficiently, and offer product lines that are similar to those of their rival commercial banks. However, the longer-term commercial viability of these banks' initial strategic goals in the modern era remains an open question. As we saw

in the last area, society at large and government may now be

expected to make a more sure interest in such socially and monetarily positive strategies. Asymmetric information, on the other hand, is the second of our economic concerns for the time being.

The advanced financial reasoning for banks and banking is made sense of

to a great extent in the corpus of data financial matters. Asymmetric information is a fundamental issue in information economics. The latter occurs when one party to a transaction has more information than the other (like a potential borrower applying for a bank loan). Adverse selection and moral hazard are two issues that arise whenever these conditions are present. More risky and unstable transactions will increasingly take the lead if these issues are not dealt with appropriately. Banks are one of the most effective ways to assess, evaluate, and monitor credit risks in contemporary financial systems. As "delegated monitors" of their depositors, banks are viewed as providing "signals" to financial markets regarding the creditworthiness of borrowers. Although techniques like regulation, collateral, and net worth are other ways to reduce asymmetric information problems, banks are viewed economically as being particularly important in this process (Mishkin, 1997).

It's possible that this significant body of economics literature, which is used to explain contemporary banking, has a direct bearing on the issues of financial exclusion. Asymmetry of information raises the issue of whether financial exclusion can be "explained" by itself. To put it another way, do the financially disadvantaged suffer as a result of banks' lack of knowledge about risk and return-based pricing?

The last option incorporate any applicable credit risk moderation procedures that

140 Monetary Rejection

may be attainable and financial to send in the event that the full credit risk profile of the borrower was known ex risk to the bank.

There are something like two potential guesses one could raise. One reason is that the world's banking markets are inefficient due to the asymmetry of information between banks and potential borrowers, the financially disadvantaged. This is the sort of contention progressed by Rothschild

what's more, Stiglitz (1976) in a commended article on the protection market. In this setting, they demonstrate that insurance markets are "pareto inefficient": That is, there is a possibility that one party in this market will benefit more than another without hurting anyone else.

However, the insurance market will not capitalize on this potential gain because the participants will not have access to all of the relevant information. Broome (1989) uses a straightforward two-person game theory model to achieve the same result: See Chakravarty (2004b) as well.

Asymmetry of information between the financially disadvantaged and banks appears to be confirmed by these theoretical results. Obviously, there are some complicated hypothetical

furthermore, reasonable (our fundamental concern) issues. Who should shoulder the "search and monitoring" costs of filling this information gap? This is an obvious practical issue. Better and more complete information (also known as "costly state verification") about the financially excluded is an obvious desiderata for assisting in the alleviation of financial exclusion; they are additionally liable to

be moderately costly. There is unquestionably an "information gap" between financial disadvantaged individuals and banks. According to our survey, there is also a lack of information regarding the impact of various bank actions on overcoming financial exclusion.

The fact that what may be in a bank's best, profit-maximizing interest may not necessarily be in society's (or "the world's") best, value-maximizing interest is another theoretical issue that has clear practical implications: In the literature on international capital flow and related bank regulation, this kind of issue is well-known: Kim, for instance (1993, chs. 2 & 12). All of these are significant theoretical and policy issues.

In addition, there is a dearth of data in these crucial areas. However, these considerations also bring us to the possibility of statistical discrimination, our third area of concern.

According to Rothschild and Stiglitz (1976), do current credit scoring models of potential bank borrowers effectively discriminate against particular customer groups due to "information deficiency" or "imperfect efficiency"? Chakravarty (2004a & b) investigates this because it is relevant to the current context and has direct practical implications.

European Strategy on Monetary Rejection and Bank Procedures 141

The contention runs like this: Since they ultimately make the system more effective (in a SWM sense) than it was before, the changes in the banking industry brought about by deregulation and other forces of the free market are inherently beneficial to society. Greater banks, more thought financial frameworks, staff cuts and branch terminations are each of the a whiz

some portion of this equivalent, 'esteem improving' process. Technological advancements also make this last process and related trends like branch closures and staff reductions easier. These not just assistance to work on a bank's gamble

the executives capacities, they likewise render the topographical area of

a branch less significant. "At a distance," data can be gathered, stored, and processed. Since technology can do everything "at a distance" and at a lower cost than branches and staff could do before "on the ground," banks are generally more efficient—which is a good thing—and no customers should be disadvantaged by the branch and staff reductions in some locations.

In today's world, there is a concern that customers in "desertified" areas will face discrimination due to their location. This is an unexpected sort of separation in comparison to that of measurable

separation based on the reliability of candidates

(instead of on their area fundamentally). Since it is based on objective, market-determined criteria, the latter is presumably "acceptable" in this world, and such discrimination is the price of economic efficiency.

Segregation based on geographic area, nonetheless, isn't

very much established in this sense: it draws nearer to 'redlining' and other, more questionable types of separation. Chakravarty (2004a) contends that

hypothesis, upheld by study proof, recommends that individual contacts

(branch and loaning official closeness) play a data handling

job (of purported 'delicate data') in the arrangement of credit and other

monetary administrations. So, the nature of data that banks use in handling loaning demands in fringe regions would be upgraded if

the banks were locked in more (in nearer actual closeness) with these

regions. By definition, "knowing your applicant" and "knowing the local market" are even more important in this type of lending.

To summarize, banks' value-maximizing behavior results in "discrimination" in lending based on business criteria. This is the result of business necessity in and of itself; In the sense of "redlining," it does not reflect any kind of prejudice. This sort of loaning action, however, may well

fuel the fringe idea of the local economy. Innovation

may likewise assist with working with this equivalent monetary cycle.

However, Chakravarty's (2000a) research emphasizes

that as banks reduce 142 Financial Exclusion their branches and staff, information may become "noisier" under these conditions. Despite the fact that it has yet to be statistically tested, there appear to be good reasons to believe that this is a real issue.

Berger et al. (2004), for instance, conduct a literature review on bank lending to SMEs and find, among other things, that big banks, which lend over longer distances, are less likely to extend relationship credit to SMEs. The apparent risk of lending to certain household groups and smaller businesses may be increased as a result of occurrences of this kind.

According to Chakravarty (2004a, p. 27), the government should "encourage organizational forms that have a stake in the local community," as he puts it. He likewise underlines the requirement for public activity pointed toward empowering and supporting such foundations. In addition, it is emphasized that regions require information of a higher quality and greater depth, as well as the impact of bank lending in these regions.

The empirical evidence on the kind of particular issues that we just talked about is very "spotty" and heavily influenced by the United States. Avery et al

(2004) inspect the likely expenses of not integrating situational

information into buyer credit assessments; these sorts of information incorporate the

monetary climate in which shoppers live or work. Avery et al.'s (2004) empirical tests strongly suggest that a person's tendency to default on a new loan is influenced by their situation. The economic effects of small business credit scoring (SBCS) are investigated by Berger et al. (2002). Their findings, for example, suggest that SBCS might make it possible for some big banks to lend more money to at least some groups of small businesses. They additionally pose the inquiry whether little US banks

have lost a significant similar benefit to huge banks on the grounds that

of SBCS. In a later report, Berger et al (2004) survey the writing and

affirm that the information from created nations by and large help the

view that enormous banks are 'burdened' in SME loaning: that is, compared to smaller banks, they devote a significantly smaller portion of their assets to SME loans. Obviously, more definite and expanded investigation into these sorts of regions is required in Europe.

The last region that we noted toward the beginning of this segment is the job of

monetary turn of events (and various types of monetary turn of events)

in provincial monetary re-age. Numerous theoretical and empirical tests have been conducted on the connection between financial growth and economic expansion. For instance, Al-Yousif (2002) discovers that economic growth and financial development are correlated in developing nations. His

results likewise support the World Bank (and others) view that the connection between monetary development and monetary improvement can't be

summed up across nations in light of the fact that monetary approaches will generally be country explicit.

European Arrangement on Monetary Rejection and Bank Methodologies 143

At provincial and bank loaning levels, the experimental writing (particularly European) is more inadequate. When Carbó Valverde and Rodrguez Fernández (2004) looked at a sample of Spanish banks from 1993 to 1999, they found that regional financial deepening was predicted by economic growth. In addition, they discovered that, in comparison to other forms of bank specialization, bank lending specialization appears to be a major obstacle to financial regional growth. In a worldwide

examination of local area banking and financial execution, Berger et

al (2004) found that more noteworthy portions of the

overall industry and productivity positions of

little, private and locally possessed banks are related with better

monetary execution. They focus on one aspect of the financial system in this study: the economic impact of community banks' health in comparison to other banks.

Conclusions The current European financial exclusion scenario has been summarized and synthesised in this chapter. The creating

European government strategy reactions affirm that monetary rejection is an undeniably significant region. Currently many banks and

banking areas have started to foster different reactions to these difficulties. Last but not least, we looked into how economic and related empirical testing contributed and played a role. 144 Financial Exclusion 2 A major international conference hosted by the World Bank and the World Savings Banks Institute in Brussels in October 2004 reaffirmed the increasing importance and policy concern with financial exclusion. Our conclusion here was that there is a practical need for additional research related to the study of financial exclusion in order to help inform the policy debate. World Bank and the WSBI, 2004).

8 Financial Exclusion in Developing Countries

Introduction

The topics covered in this chapter focus on financial exclusion in developing nations. Many equals between drives are being made

in the created and creating world to urge portions of society to

utilize monetary administrations. Evidently, a significant portion of the population in many developing nations lacks access to financial services, and many of these nations' financial systems and institutions are significantly underdeveloped. The main characteristics of financial exclusion in developing nations are the focus of this chapter, which also looks at various mechanisms that have been suggested to promote financial inclusion, including the role of informal financial networks and various microfinance initiatives.

Reference all through the part is made to the more extensive money and improvement writing that likewise stresses the advancement of the monetary administrations industry as a significant driver of financial development.

Highlights of monetary rejection in agricultural nations

The issue of monetary avoidance is obviously disparate in industrialized

furthermore, non-industrial nations in any event, for two fundamental reasons:

• The vast majority of people in developing nations are affected by financial exclusion, which is strongly linked to poverty and a lack of capital resources. As a result, there is a finished set of institutional variables that ought to be considered as wellsprings of

monetary rejection in these nations; furthermore,

- Emerging nations show an essentially lower level of monetary

advancement contrasted with industrialized economies. Because of this, 145 countries' financial exclusion is linked to financial underdevelopment, and it is necessary to demonstrate how important finance is for growth and reducing poverty.

Holden and Prokopenko (2001) state that a variety of public and private sources of financial underdevelopment can be identified. According to the public authority viewpoint, the state-possessed

model of monetary framework will in general rule in generally creating nations. In this specific circumstance, there have been a few episodes of political entrepreneurial way of behaving that have brought about an inconsistent circulation of assets. Since politicians have been unable to find adequate mechanisms to encourage the managers of state-owned financial institutions to run banks and other financial firms in an efficient manner, market-based incentive schemes that have been incorporated into state-dominated financial systems typically have not functioned as intended.

When assessing the government's role in financial underdevelopment, regulatory issues are also significant. First of all, many developing nations lack adequate financial infrastructure. These nations have not yet implemented many of the fundamental components of modern financial systems, such as entry requirements for banking sectors, deposit insurance, functional separation of financial institutions, solvency regulations, and lender of last resort facilities.

In addition, Holden and Prokopenko (2001) demonstrated that the reliance on direct monetary policy instruments like interest rate control has harmed credit availability and financial development. However, it has been demonstrated that the shift toward indirect instruments (such as open market operations or reserve requirements) has been less restrictive for financial development in many nations over the past two decades.

With respects the confidential area, the job of monetary organizations is especially applicable in emerging nations, taking into account the select

reliance (when accessible) of most families and firms on bank

supporting and the shortfall of options in the capital business sectors. It

ought to be noticed that the conventional checking and screening elements of monetary delegates is challenging to execute in these economies, because of the shortfall of proficient data components

furthermore, an exceptionally restricted scope of venture projects as well as certifications/

insurance. Since "insiders," or depositors, have no incentive to act prudently, the adverse selection issue takes center stage in many financial systems of developing nations.

146 Financial Exclusion

Another significant issue is the inadequate collection of savings by financial institutions in developing nations and the relatively low level of savings there. Also from a supply perspective, it is important to note that many financial institutions lack the necessary technological capacity to benefit from scale economies and expand branch networks. As a result, it is not surprising that many people find it difficult, if not impossible, to open a savings or current account. All things considered,

the low degree of monetary delegate advancement in these nations

can be made sense of by a wasteful inventory of administrations, a lacking

request and a serious level of self-prohibition connected with the dishonesty of possible contributors in the entire framework.

Inadequate management and regulatory frameworks are another source of inefficiencies in the banking sectors of developing nations. Above all else, credit arrangement is straightforwardly impacted by

the failure of banks to oversee credit risk. Macroeconomic instability is largely responsible for this incapacity. When banks refuse to lend to borrowers who are of low quality, this situation may lead to credit rationing.

On the other hand, assuming loaning is unreasonable, default rates can increment significantly, which, thus, will deteriorate what is happening.

Data issues are additionally exacerbated because of the presence - in

the majority of the financial areas of non-industrial nations - of unfortunate bookkeeping records that hampers credit risk the executives. Inefficiencies in credit risk assessment can also be attributed to a lack of adequate management control across bank branch networks, which occurs when managers in the head office do not have control over individual branch-level decisions.

In addition, collateral is difficult to rely on because many households in developing nations lack adequate property rights that guarantee their property's title.

Financial underdevelopment and rural economies The existence of a rural-based socioeconomic structure is one of the main causes of financial exclusion in developing nations. As a result, all institutional, regulatory, and microeconomic aspects of financial underdevelopment must be evaluated in this context because rural environments again influence the geography of financial exclusion. Wenner (2000) studies the issues of monetary turn of events and

monetary avoidance in rustic regions following the examples of a few encounters at the Between American Improvement Bank. Financial Exclusion in Developing Countries 147 Exclusion in these countries can be traced back to a number of issues that have been identified. Three of the wellsprings of monetary underdevelopment are especially pertinent to monetary avoidance: pricing and risk management in the financial intermediary industry; disparities in information;

and transaction costs that come with working in an institutional setting.

First and foremost, rural economies are characterized by high-risk strategies when it comes to pricing and risk behavior. Provincial rural business people - generally individual or little firm gatherings - normally embrace

monetary agreements that are dependent upon a serious level of (financial) changeability and typically bring about compulsory default. There are different wellsprings of changeability at this level: supply fluctuation as a result of unfavorable production conditions (weather, illness, health, equipment failure), fluctuation in input prices that raise production costs, or shifts in supply as a result of altered price expectations.

Rural households and businesses employ a variety of approaches to address these issues. To begin, they can generate credit availability from informal sources like Rotating Saving and Credit Associations (ROSCAs) by investing in social collateral. One of the most established informal financial institutions in developing nations, ROSCAs are widely used in Asia and Africa. The fundamental idea behind ROSCAs is nearly universal: a group of people meet for a series of meetings, and at each meeting, everyone contributes to a common pot. The pot is given to one individual from the gathering and this

part is then avoided from getting the pot later on gatherings

while as yet adding to the pot. Until all members have received their share, the procedure is repeated. The ROSCA may begin a new cycle or be disbanded once all members have received the pot.

Lower accessibility of credit upsets enhancement and increments

weakness to risk. The limited number of default risk mitigation mechanisms, such as collateral, available in rural economies is another risk factor. The latter entails a risk premium in credit interest rates. Additionally, establishing sufficient loan loss reserves systems is challenging. Overall, there is less risk diversification because of the limited geographic coverage of financial intermediation and the interconnected nature of many of the economic activities that will receive financing. Consequently, open doors for productive

intermediation are decreased. As a result, it does not appear that formal intermediaries are motivated to enter rural markets.

Rural markets are also particularly affected by

information asymmetries. The expense of acquiring and handling data are moreover

focal in evaluating and overseeing risk. 148 Financial Exclusion borrower quality information can mitigate screening, adverse selection, and moral hazard issues to a certain extent in light of the previously mentioned risks. Social collateral (reputation) is utilized in place of real collateral in the majority of rural settings. These tied connections are pertinent for specialists like Rosca's, town

banks and customary moneylenders. In comparison to a formal intermediary, these (informal) intermediaries obtain customer creditworthiness information more quickly and at a lower cost. As a result, informal lenders are able to identify clients with greater accuracy who will repay a loan commitment as long as the project return or household resources permit. Depositors face similar issues on the demand side because it is difficult for them to trust these intermediaries' capacity as fiduciaries.

Checking is one more component in the riddle of data deviations in rustic regions whenever screening has been finished. To avoid moral hazard incentive issues, rural lenders should invest in client behavior monitoring just like any other financial intermediary.

Be that as it may, there seem scale diseconomies related with this interaction

since formal monetary mediators find these observing expenses

intolerable, taking into account the little size of credits requested by most

rustic clients. Accordingly, contracts in view of notoriety and social vicinity comprise the fundamental substitute for formal checking in

these regions.

The third variable related with monetary avoidance in provincial areas of

agricultural nations is the job of exchange costs and the institutional setting. The significantly lower level of income and greater degree of spatial dispersion of rural clients in developing countries, in contrast to high-income clients in developed nations, results in higher transaction costs for both intermediaries and customers.

Some of the main institutional factors, such as property rights, contract enforcement, and prudential regulation and supervision, have a significant impact on transaction costs in rural areas.1 In rural areas, the absence or inefficiency of legal frameworks that secure property rights is particularly problematic. Contract enforcement represents all kinds of legal and social claims against property, including debtor's property, which is the complete definition and control of the property, and security interest, which is the right to be paid from the sale or exchange of Financial Exclusion in Developing Countries 149 1. For a survey of the implications of various legal and financial environments for economic development in both developed and developing countries, see Demirgüç-Kunt and Maksimovic (1998).

property. However, the majority of land or property registries in developing nations are lacking, making it costly, time-consuming, and risky to search for, register, and document a security interest.

Because lenders are unable to rely on public registries to

determine whether another creditor has a prior claim, lending against accounts receivable is too risky in this context.

Prudential guidelines and management are likewise inadequate as a component to address or moderate market disappointment emerging from moral risk

what's more, educational imbalances among providers and purchasers of monetary administrations. The problem of banking sector and financial system supervision in developing countries, particularly in rural areas, is primarily defined by structural controls, prudential norms, and consumer protection regulations. Underlying controls allude to advertise

section and exit, geographic limitations, solidification and the reach of administrations that monetary firms can offer. Prudential controls try to

give security to the framework by making individual monetary organizations more secure, subsequently expanding customer certainty. Information disclosure and the development of dispute resolution systems are related to consumer protection regulations. Due to the different accounting standards used in developing nations, the information provided is sometimes difficult to interpret or compare. For regulators, shareholders, and depositors, this results in non-transparency. Many developing nations have implemented capital adequacy standards, accounting reforms, and provisioning requirements, but improvements in stability remain a long way off. Why are these issues so significant in rural areas? Once more, the response is unequivocally connected with the institutional

climate.

A crucial issue is the existence of specialized financial institutions that effectively develop screening and monitoring functions for rural activities, given the characteristics of rural economies. Even though some developing nations permit financial institutions to provide only a limited range of services, many legal frameworks prohibit specialized or restricted banking. Different nations require high least

capital guidelines that favor the production of few

monetary elements instead of a huge number with low norms. These

prerequisites increment solidification in the financial area and deteriorate contest, specialization and the geographic scattering of monetary

administrations.

In contrast, a wide variety of semi-formal entities (such as credit unions, village banks, and cooperatives) and informal entities (such as supplier150 Financial Exclusion traders, ROSCAs, and moneylenders) have thrived in these rural settings despite the absence of formal financial institutions.

Rather than giving various individual advances, the utilization of gathering

credit has become normal for these organizations, which is by all accounts

more proper for guarantee obliged borrowers. Given this structure, informal providers typically have the smallest transactions, semi-formal entities have slightly larger ones, and formal financial intermediaries have the largest. Notwithstanding, as Wenner (2000)

brings up, after various cycles, exchange expenses can increment

considerably in bunch credit plans and it might become vital

to give individual credit items to keep the client base. The main reason is that there are gaps between what customers want and what products are available, which leads to more transaction costs and inefficiencies.

Information advantages due to proximity, deeper lending relationships, and greater flexibility with collateral are attributed to informal intermediaries like suppliertraders, ROSCAs, and moneylenders in comparison to formal rural financial intermediaries. In any case, there are likewise gambles related with casual go-betweens, since they have less fortunate capital levels and higher

market power. Consequently, despite lower transaction costs, they typically charge higher interest rates. In this setting, semi-formal intermediaries like credit unions, village banks, and cooperatives also benefit from some informational advantages.

Exclusion and financial development It is convenient to examine the significance of differences between developed and developing nations because financial underdevelopment and financial exclusion are strongly correlated in developing nations.

In addition, this analysis may be able to reveal connections between economic growth and financial development in developing nations. Notwithstanding, right now, it ought to be noticed that the connection among money and development might be different relying upon the

condition of monetary advancement itself. Particularly, there is a lot of debate about whether economic growth is aided by financial development or the other way around. Which way is the cause moving? Is it similar in created and creating economies?

There have been a few drives - especially from establishments such

as the World Bank, Global Money related Asset (IMF) and the OECD

- attempting to unravel the significance of monetary framework improvement

Monetary Avoidance in Non-industrial Nations 151

to monetary development in industrialized and created nations. This area sums up this writing and points:

• To show the component of the issue of monetary underdevelopment in emerging nations contrasted with industrialized nations.

The primary objective is to examine national data on financial penetration and the finance-growth nexus; • To demonstrate that financial inclusion is promoted by financial development, which not only benefits the poor but also the rich.

The finance-growth nexus and financial underdevelopment In recent years, a number of studies have assessed the level of financial development and its effect on economic growth across countries. The majority of these studies have examined processes of financial dependence and deepening, and the distinction between these two concepts is crucial for illustrating differences between developed and developing nations.

Monetary extending is the degree of advancement and development of

conventional and contemporary monetary administrations. A bank credit variable is used in the majority of international studies. According to King and Levine (1993), financial liberalization has a positive impact on bank efficiency by lowering intermediation costs and has a positive and significant correlation with bank credit development and faster economic growth. In a similar vein, in the early stages of industrial development, Rousseau and Wachtel (1998) suggest that financial development boosts long-term economic growth. Rioja and Valev (2004) also find a positive relationship between growth and financial development, but the significance of this relationship varies depending on the starting point. In agricultural nations,

monetary extending is oftentimes connected with monetary progression processes.

Even if financial flows are increased in these nations as a result of liberalization, greater financial penetration is not guaranteed. The degree to which savings are channeled through the financial system to provide investment financing is measured by financial penetration. Financial penetration and deepening are often used together, but penetration is not always guaranteed and liberalization is not always effective. Even though more formal microfinance programs are also rapidly developing, informal mechanisms like ROSCA's continue to exist in 152 Financial Exclusion developing countries due to these differences. For example, a lot of people won't even be willing to do any kind of formal business; instead, they prefer to use informal lenders to get money for their needs (Fry, 1995, chapter). 6).

The degree to which households and businesses rely on bank financing to carry out their investment projects is related to financial dependence.

Since households and businesses in these nations rely heavily on (formal or informal) intermediaries, financial dependence is especially relevant in developing economies. Recent research suggests that legal and institutional factors may also significantly contribute to the explanation of bank deepening and the growth effects of financial dependence. It has been demonstrated that the recent liberalization of bank activities—with a tendency toward broad banking in the majority of financial systems—improves the efficiency of financial intermediation and their contribution to economic growth2.

Printed in Great Britain
by Amazon